OLIVER SUNDEW, TOOTH FAIRY

Oliver may have a damaged wing, but he's determined to be a tooth fairy like his friends.

Sam McBratney was a teacher for many years and is now a full-time writer. The winner of a Bass Ireland Arts Prize and twice winner of the Bisto Award, he has written many books, stories and radio plays for adults and children, including the Walker titles *Art, You're Magic!*, *The Green Kids, Flash Eddie and the Big Bad Wolf, In Crack Willow Wood* and the million-selling picture book *Guess How Much I Love You* (shortlisted for the Kurt Maschler Award and the British Book Awards: Illustrated Children's Book of the Year). Married with three grown-up children and an ancient tortoise, Sam McBratney lives in County Antrim, Northern Ireland.

Dom Mansell has illustrated several books for children, including *The Selfish Giant* (shortlisted for the Mother Goose Award), *Judy the Bad Fairy, My Great Grandpa, Terrormazia,* and his own story *My Old Teddy*. He lives in Barnsley, South Yorkshire.

Books by the same author

Art, You're Magic!
In Crack Willow Wood
The Green Kids

For younger readers

Guess How Much I Love You

SAM McBRATNEY

OLIVER SUNDEW
tooth fairy

Illustrations by Dom Mansell

WALKER BOOKS
AND SUBSIDIARIES
LONDON • BOSTON • SYDNEY

First published 1995 by Walker Books Ltd,
87 Vauxhall Walk, London SE11 5HJ

This edition published 1996

2 4 6 8 10 9 7 5 3 1

Text © 1995 Sam McBratney
Illustrations © 1995 Dom Mansell

This book has been typeset in ITC Garamond.

Printed in England

British Library Cataloguing in Publication Data
A catalogue record for this book
is available from the British Library.

ISBN 0-7445-4375-4

CONTENTS

GOOD NEWS

It was market day in Oliver Sundew's home town. Mr Nimble Jay was about to make a speech from the balcony of the Town Hall. However, the place was so crowded and so noisy that no one could hear him.

"Now listen to me, all you people," he said loudly. "I have some news. Important news, so be quiet and open your ears!" And he glared at them all – especially the Fiddler, who was making more noise than anyone else. The crowd fell silent.

"That's better," said Mr Nimble Jay. "I'm here to tell you that a tooth has just come out in a faraway city. It's a top tooth, a front tooth, the very best sort you can get, and we are sending a team of tooth fairies to bring it back. What do you think about that?"

The crowd was delighted.
Everybody loved the excitement of
a tooth hunt, so it was hardly a
surprise when dancing broke out all
over the tooth-cobbled square.

14

Hats flew in the air and the Fiddler
lifted his fiddle to his chin and played
more loudly than ever. Oliver Sundew
stood on his frog's back and cheered
until he was hoarse.

When at last a hush
fell over the
marketplace, Mr
Nimble Jay was
able to continue.
"Four of us will
leave to bring back the tooth.
But remember – this is going to be
dangerous."

"If you want to be chosen to come on my tooth hunt, bring yourself to the Town Hall tomorrow morning. Do not apply if you are afraid of magpies or giant spiders...

"or anything else that gobbles fairies up. Tomorrow morning, nine o'clock. And don't be late."

That was the end of Mr Nimble Jay's speech. Oliver Sundew climbed on board his frog and rode home. *Magpies and spiders don't scare me,* he thought. *If I go to the Town Hall tomorrow morning, maybe Mr Nimble Jay will pick me to go and get that tooth!*

OLIVER JOINS THE QUEUE

When Oliver arrived at the Town
Hall early next morning, there was
already a long queue waiting to see
Mr Nimble Jay. Oliver saw two of
his friends. One was called
Cornpepper Rose and the other,
Henry B.

Cornpepper Rose said, "Hiya, Olly."

Henry B said, "Do you want to be a tooth fairy, too?"

Then another voice spoke. It belonged to Martin Goosegrass. "What are you doing here, Oliver Sundew? Nimble Jay will never pick you to be one of his tooth fairies. He would rather go on his own than pick you."

"He might not pick you either, Martin Goosegrass," said Oliver.

The queue began to move. Soon it was Oliver's turn to go in and see Mr Nimble Jay, who was a burly-looking fellow with a big red face.

"So you want to be a tooth fairy, boy?"

"Yes, I do, sir."

"Are you afraid of spiders and beetles and creepy-crawlies like that?" he asked.

"Not a bit," said Oliver.

"Scorpions, then? What about leaping trout and the Kingfisher Blue?"

"Well, I don't like them very much," said Oliver, "but I'm not afraid of them."

"Good. Can you fly fast?"

Oliver Sundew paused. As a matter of fact, flying gave him problems. "You see, sir," he explained, "I flew into a candle when I was small and I've got only one good wing."

"Then you won't do!" declared
Mr Nimble Jay. "You just won't do.
What would happen if you got
chased by a blasted robin or a
jenny-wren? They'd eat you. Gobble
you. Peck, swallow and *whoosh* –
no more Oliver Sundew. Sorry, lad,
until you've got two good wings
you'll just not do as a tooth fairy."

"I'm a very good swimmer, sir," said Oliver.

"Swimming's no good," cried Mr Nimble Jay. "But there is something you can do for me. Run over to the bank and get me a coin. Tell the bank manager it's for a front top tooth in perfect condition, and I want it now."

THE ONE-POUND COIN

Naturally Oliver Sundew was very disappointed, but he hurried across the tooth-cobbled square to the bank. The manager wore a stiff white collar and he looked down his extra-long nose at Oliver.

"Hmm. A top front tooth, eh?"
he said. "It might be bad, you know.
Children nowadays eat so many
horrible sticky sweets. We don't pay
so much for a bad tooth, you know."

"This is a perfect tooth," said
Oliver. "It has no fillings."

"Then I suppose I shall have to give you a one-pound coin. Oh, well."

A few moments later Oliver came out of the bank with a one-pound coin, which he wheeled along like a hoop.

Already the square was bustling with activity, for the tooth hunt was about to begin. Flags were flying, and the Fiddler fiddled madly in the street. When Mr Nimble Jay arrived, Oliver was pleased to see that his friends Cornpepper Rose and Henry B had been chosen to go on the tooth hunt.

Then he noticed someone else.
Martin Goosegrass was going, too.
No doubt this was because he could
read maps and fly very fast, even in
the pouring rain.

"I told you so, Oliver Sundew,"
said Martin Goosegrass nastily. "I
said Nimble Jay would never pick
you and I was right – you're just not
the proper sort to be a tooth fairy."

It was time to go. Nimble Jay,
Cornpepper Rose, Henry B and
Martin Goosegrass rose into the air,
and beneath them, suspended in a
large net, the sparkling coin swayed
to and fro.

Oliver was feeling quite sad, so he jumped on his frog's back and hopped home. *I can't read maps,* thought Oliver. *I can't fly very fast and I'm not really much good at anything, except for swimming. Toads alive, I should have been a fish!*

DEEP, DEEP WATER

The hours went by. In the tooth-cobbled square, crowds waited anxiously for news of the tooth hunt. Some said that an owl had swallowed Cornpepper Rose for supper. Others said that a cat had pounced on Henry B.

I hope it isn't true, thought Oliver Sundew, who was just as worried as everyone else.

Then, amid a great stir of excitement, Martin Goosegrass flew into the marketplace. "We can't get the tooth!" he told the crowd breathlessly. "It's way down deep in a glass of water – you never saw a tooth in so much water."

The crowd let loose mighty groans
and sighs. Fire and oil and water –
these were the things which fairies
hated most.

Martin Goosegrass spoke again.
"Nimble Jay sent me back for somebody who isn't afraid of deep water."

That silenced the crowd
completely. None of them could
bear the thought of wet wings –
most of them refused to fly in a
shower of rain.

Then one voice
spoke up clearly.
"I'm not afraid
of water.
I'll get the
tooth."

Martin Goosegrass turned to face the speaker. He could hardly believe his eyes. It was Oliver Sundew. "You? But you've got only one wing."

"I've got one wing and a half," Oliver corrected him. "And I can fly a little. In fact, I can fly a lot if I take rests. And I can swim."

Somebody shouted from the crowd. "He's right, you know, I've seen him. By the toads, he can swim better than a tadpole."

So they told Martin Goosegrass
that Oliver was the one he must
take back with him. "Well, you'll
have to be quick," he warned.
"People will be waking up in three
hours' time."

43

And Oliver knew what that meant. If a human being saw a fairy, that fairy vanished. No one knew why or where to, but the thought of being seen by an early-morning milkman was enough to make a fairy shiver until his wings fell off.

WONDERFUL OLIVER SUNDEW

Away they went. Oliver flew as quickly as he could, but because he had to stop and rest many times, there were milk bottles on the doorstep when they arrived.

They tumbled through the letterbox – which Mr Nimble Jay had
cleverly propped open with a
lollipop stick – and flew up the stairs.

"What kept you?" snapped Mr
Nimble Jay. "Never mind, I haven't
time to listen. Come over here, boy,
have a look at this tooth. How are
we ever going to get our hands on
that?"

Pale and beautifully smooth, the
perfect tooth lay at the bottom of an
enormous glass of water.
Toads alive!
thought Oliver.
It was a long
way down.

Toads alive

"I'll have a go, sir," he said.
And now, Oliver Sundew
crouched on the
rim of the tall-
standing glass.
His wings
twinkled
momentarily,
then flattened
along his
back as he
dived head
first into the
water.

Down he went – down,
down in a stream of
bubbles to where
the perfect tooth lay
like a gorgeous pearl.
Air leaked through
his lips with a
blurble-burble.
Roaring winds,
and the thumping
drumbeat of
his heart,
seemed to
fill his ears.

Then his hands hit bottom and closed around the tooth. As his head began to fill up with light, he felt the rope tighten at his waist.

Mr Nimble Jay was shouting
outside the glass. "Heave! Get him
up there, quick! Has he got it? Did
he get that tooth?"

When Oliver Sundew came out of the water, he held up the tooth for them all to see.

"You are wonderful, Oliver Sundew!" cried Cornpepper Rose.

And she immediately danced a jig
with Henry B. They wished that the
Fiddler had been there to play one
of his tunes.

It was time to go home. Mr
Nimble Jay wiped up the water
which had spilled from Oliver's
wings, and then there was just one
more thing to be done.

They dropped the shining new
coin into the glass of water.

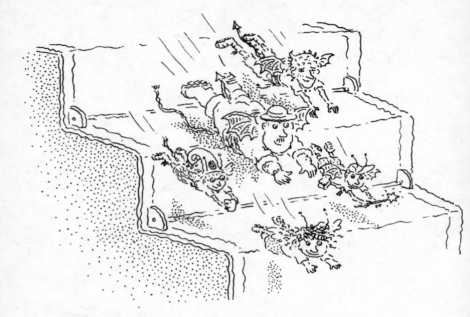

Down the stairs they flew,

out through the letterbox,

up between the telephone wires,
and into the rising sun.

Only five minutes after they
had gone, the postman arrived
at the house.

He wondered why the
letterbox had been propped open
with a lollipop stick.

MORE WALKER SPRINTERS
For You to Enjoy